DALE EARNHARDT

The Intimidator

by

Kathy Persinger

SPORTS PUBLISHING INC.

www.SportsPublishingInc.com

www.thatsracin.com

© 2001 Sports Publishing Inc.
All rights reserved.

Series editor: Mike Persinger
Director of Production: Susan M. McKinney
Cover design: Christina Cary
Coordinating editor: Claudia Mitroi
Photo editor: Sandy Arneson
Photos: *The Charlotte Observer*

ISBN: 1-58261-427-X

SPORTS PUBLISHING INC.
www.SportsPublishingInc.com

Printed in the United States.

Contents

Acknowledgments

The sport of stock car racing was officially born on June 19, 1949, when the first race of what is now Winston Cup was run in Charlotte, North Carolina.

On February 18, 2001, the nucleus of NASCAR racing died.

Dale Earnhardt, the world's most popular driver, was killed instantly when his No. 3 Goodwrench Chevrolet crashed on the last lap of the Daytona 500. Across the country, flags were lowered to half-staff. Memorial services were held. Mountains of flowers and mementos accumulated in front of the Earnhardt shop in Mooresville, North Carolina.

"It's like losing Elvis," one fan said.

This book tells a little bit about the man in black who took that No. 3 car for a ride to seven Winston Cup championships and 76 checkered flags.

And it is about a man who maintained his true identity amidst the fame, the money, the burden of being an international celebrity. Dale was, truly, just a regular guy. To be around him and talk with him was like being with an old friend. He was a husband, a father, a son, an uncle. He kept his perspective, and that's something to be admired.

Thank you, Dale.

"Thank yous" for this book also go to the friendly people at the Cabarrus Regional Chamber of Commerce in Kannapolis, North Carolina, and to the residents of Sedan Avenue, who are clinging to an irreplaceable piece of that city's history and allowing it to thrive.

Thanks to Lowe's Motor Speedway president H. A. "Humpy" Wheeler, an expert on the racing business. Thanks to long-time *Charlotte Observer* racing writer Tom Higgins, always good for an amusing Earnhardt story, and to the photographers at *The Observer* who provided the pictures for this book.

Thanks to Dale's public relations representative, John "J. R." Rhodes.

And a special thanks to the late Ralph Earnhardt, who let his son in on the secret of his special talent, taught him how to run the race and taught him how to win it while still being a gentleman. Sports needs more people like that.

Thank you to Dale Earnhardt, Jr., who is carrying on a tradition of excellence.

And finally, thank you to my husband, Mike, and children Christopher, Sarah and Tyler, who have understood and endured this project.

Introduction

Here's Your Future—Love, Dad

If there was one thread that connected all that NASCAR superstar Dale Earnhardt became —from country boy in rural Kannapolis, North Carolina, to international celebrity—it was his father, Ralph Earnhardt.

Ralph was a race driver, running Grand National and late-model sportsman cars around dirt tracks in the Carolinas and other parts of the South on weekends. He took his home-built cars on a 23-year trip that produced more than 500 victories, and through every mile of it Dale was there.

He was there on the concrete garage floor as a toddler, playing with toy cars while Ralph worked on the big engines.

He was there on weekends, standing on the front of the tow truck, straining to see over the crowds as Ralph blew dust on the windshields of Banjo Matthews and other top drivers of the 1950s.

He was there for the two decades of championships and learned not only what it was like to be a winner but also what it was like to be devoted to home and family.

Ralph Earnhardt died in September 1973 while working on a car in his backyard garage. But Dale, who was 22 then, loved his daddy so much that he wouldn't let him disappear.

Dale was determined to be a race car driver, too. "I guess it took Daddy 10 years to know what he was doing," Dale said back then. "I hope I progress as rapidly as he did."

No problem.

Dale entered some Grand National races in 1976. His determination and speed, along with his friendly attitude and willingness to learn, got him noticed by the more established names on the circuit. In 1979, he started 27 races, had 11 top-five finishes and was Rookie of the Year. He also won $264,086, a fortune in Ralph's day.

Dale went on to win 76 Winston Cup races before 2001 and would be Winston Cup champion in 1980, 1986, 1987, 1990, 1991, 1993 and 1994.

He has fans around the world. His picture and that of his No. 3 Goodwrench Chevrolet are on every type of souvenir imaginable.

Each race, thousands of fans came just to cheer for him. He made more money than he could ever spend. His family owns 1,000 acres in Mooresville, North Carolina, which he lived on and farmed. There is a huge garage complex and showroom out front on the highway for all the world to see.

Yet for all that happened, one thread remained: his love for his daddy.

On the race track, Dale was fierce. Off it, he was quiet, almost shy, and totally devoted to his wife, Teresa, and children Kerry, Kelley, Dale Jr. and Taylor Nicole. He was extremely close to his mother, Martha, and his brothers and sisters. He was, as they say, down-home.

When it comes down to it, Dale Earnhardt was a family man who just happened to drive race cars.

Ralph Earnhardt would have liked that.

Dale finally gets to hoist the Daytona 500 trophy in Victory Lane after winning the race on his 20th attempt. (Charlotte Observer/Jeff Siner)

Finally, Daytona

It was February 15, 1998, and NASCAR superstar Dale Earnhardt, nicknamed "the Intimidator," was reclining in his black race car at Daytona International Speedway awaiting the start of the Daytona 500. A deliberate competitor who piloted a four-wheeled, swerving runaway train for a living, his blue-eyed gaze would demand, "Get out of my way, or else." Dale did not earn his nickname by accident, although some say he partially earned it by causing them.

Still, after two decades of stock car racing, Dale had not won the big one at the Florida track. Close, yes, but no checkered flag.

"I have been passed on the last lap, I have run out of gas and I have cut a tire," Dale said of some of his previous Daytona 500s.

Plus, he had gone 59 races—nearly two seasons—without a win anywhere, and the media were continuously asking him the same question: "Hey, Dale, what about Daytona?"

Never mind that he had won 30 other races at the 2.5-mile track. The 500 was elusive.

But on this day, 20 became Dale Earnhardt's lucky number. In his 20th attempt, Dale won the Daytona 500. He won it after stopping for fuel and right-side tires with 30 laps to go. He won it after the yellow caution flag flew on Lap 199 of 200 following a collision between drivers Jimmy Spencer and John Andretti.

And he won it with the third-fastest time ever —averaging 172.712 miles per hour.

"I cried a little bit in the race car on the way to the checkered flag," Dale said. "Well, maybe not cried, but at least my eyes watered up.

"It was my time. I don't care how we won it, but we won it."

There was a 180,000-spectator standing ovation.

More than 100 crew members from other teams jumped the pit wall to congratulate him as he drove to Victory Lane.

It was the biggest win of his life, and it needed the biggest celebration, which meant . . . doughnuts.

Dale pulled into the infield grass and spun his No. 3 Goodwrench Chevrolet around until the skid marks looked as if he had landscaped a "3" in the turf.

Dale stands with other NASCAR drivers (left to right) Jimmy Spencer, Michael Waltrip, Dale Jarrett, Sterling Marlin and Terry Labonte during driver introductions for the 1998 Daytona 500 . (Charlotte Observer/Jeff Siner)

Fans ran from the stands to collect pieces of the grass and dirt and stow them away in their nearest safety-deposit boxes—their coolers.

Later, in the press box, Dale pulled a toy monkey out of his shirt and shouted, "I'm here, and I got that monkey off my back!"

Said teammate Mike Skinner, "You're the man. You're a baaad man!"

Dale and his wife, Teresa, celebrate in 1998 after his first victory at the Daytona 500. (Charlotte Observer/ Jeff Siner)

"He's Going to Be a Star"

I t wasn't the most impressive of starts, but it got him noticed.

In 1976, Dale ran a couple of races on the Grand National circuit. In May that year, the rookie qualified 25th for the World 600 at Charlotte. In November, in the Dixie 500 at Atlanta International Speedway, he flipped his car four times, completely mangled the metal and had to be extracted from the crumpled heap. He escaped with only a slightly cut hand.

Not exactly trophy material. But Dale's attitude and competitive desire had already caught the attention of one of racing's most well-known and influential people—Humpy Wheeler.

"It has been a long time since I've seen a youngster so determined, so hungry," Wheeler said back then. "If nothing happens to sour his attitude, I think he's going to be a star within a few years, and a big one."

A quarter of a century later, Wheeler still remembers the start of Dale's career.

"Great drivers can see things other people can't," he said. "We don't have a test for it yet, but I feel he had those kind of eyes."

Those eyes were focused on stardom, and the National Association of Stock Car Auto Racing was about to be taken for a 25-year roller-coaster ride.

It wasn't always easy for Dale. Wheeler recalls a story from the mid-1970s when Dale was almost out of money and had just wrecked his race car.

Wheeler told him, "Since you don't have any money, you need to go backward. See if Robert Gee will give you a ride in his dirt car."

Gee was a legend in NASCAR, the guy who began to perfect body sculpting in race cars.

Dale got a job, but there was a catch. Before Dale could drive the car, he had to help work in Gee's body shop.

"Well, a week later, after Earnhardt started working, they were painting a car for Darrell Waltrip," Wheeler said. "Everything was orange. Their lungs were orange, too."

Wheeler visited the body shop. That dirt car still was sitting there, untouched.

"I know that car's over there, but I'm not going to let him have it until he gets to be a better painter," Robert Gee said.

Three weeks later, Dale won a race in that car.

Soon, he was headed back to the Winston Cup series.

In 1979, Dale started 27 races. He had just one victory, the Southeastern 500 at Bristol, Tennessee, but he won four poles and had 17 top-10 finishes, 11 of those in the top five. And he won $264,086.

He was Rookie of the Year.

And people were starting to talk.

His crew chief, J.C. "Jake" Elder: "Dale can be as good as anybody I ever worked with."

Driver Cale Yarborough: "Dale's got about as much potential as anybody I've seen in a long time. If he doesn't rush it, he'll make it big."

Driver Darrell Waltrip: "I saw how The Boy run at Daytona, and I was impressed. For someone that's been doing this as long as I have, you just have a way of telling raw talent."

As much of an impact as Dale was making among his peers, there was someone else he wanted more to impress.

"I know that somewhere there's a fellow that's got a big smile and is mighty, mighty proud and even more happy than I am, if that's possible," Dale said after his Bristol win.

He was referring to his daddy.

Dale put his signature on many Winston Cup races. (Charlotte Observer/Jeff Siner)

1980:
Wheels of Fortune

Dale opened the 1980s with a rush. In 31 races in 1980, he had five victories —at Atlanta; Bristol; Nashville; Martinsville, Virginia; and his home base, Charlotte. He had 23 top-10 finishes and won $588,926.

He also won the Winston Cup championship, taking the title by 19 points after finishing fifth in the *L.A. Times* 500 at Ontario (Calif.) Motor Speedway on Nov. 15. It was then that he gave credit to his religion.

"We were lucky, and I really believe we had some help from a pretty high source," he said. "You can prepare as carefully as possible and run as hard as you can, but in the end, having faith and belief counts for an awful lot."

It was the first of seven Winston Cup titles for Dale, 29, and he outraced the likes of stars Bobby Allison, Cale Yarborough and Benny Parsons to get it, even though he went through two crew-chief changes during the season.

He also got about $300,000 in bonus money and celebrated with a victory party in Las Vegas with his younger brothers, Randy and Danny. They stayed in a big hotel suite with ceiling-high mirrors, a spiral staircase, a piano and three bedrooms. The place was huge.

"Gol-l-l-l-e-e-e," Dale said when he saw it. "This is as big as most houses back home."

But while Dale was well positioned on the track, off the track was a different story.

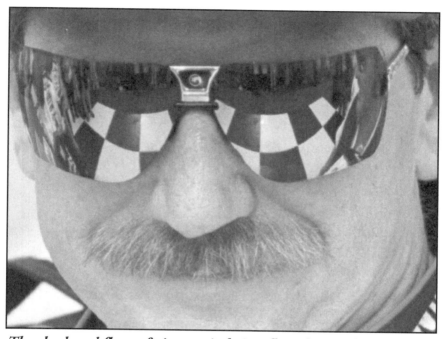

The checkered floor of victory circle is reflected in Dale's sunglasses after he won the second of two Gatorade 125 races at Daytona International Speedway. (Charlotte Observer/Jeff Siner)

And Now, a Word from Our Sponsor

A NASCAR team must have a talented driver, of course, but it also has a team owner, a crew chief, several crew members who work in the pits on race day and many people who work in the race shop every day building and fine-tuning the race cars.

After each race season, drivers and teams often evaluate their progress and decide whether they want to stay together for another year or change teams.

"I hate this time of year every season," Dale's former team owner, Bud Moore, said in 1983. "It gets aggravating and confusing. Why, it's been like ring-around-the-rosey around here."

Dale did his share of switching in the 1980s.

In January 1980, he signed a five-year contract with Osterlund Racing, based in the Derita area of Charlotte. "Talk about job security," he said then, "I've got it."

But in May that year, crew chief Jake Elder quit the Osterlund team and was replaced by Doug Richert.

In February of 1981, Richert was replaced by Dale Inman, which was strange because Inman is Richard Petty's cousin and had worked with the Petty team since the 1950s.

"It's the biggest shock wave to hit our sport in many, many years," driver Benny Parsons said. "It's something I guess no one in racing ever thought they'd see."

It didn't last long.

In June 1981, coal-mining executive Jim Stacy bought Osterlund Racing and fired six employees. Dale, who was sponsored by Wrangler jeans, was in a bind. Should he stay or leave?

He made up his mind by August 3.

"Jim," he said, "you're a nice fellow, and I haven't got a thing against you. But I've got to do something I should have done when the team changed ownership. I'm going to quit."

By the next day, Dale had a new team. Thing is, it was ring-around-the-rosey all over again. Dale took over the driver's seat from Richard Childress, who had been building and driving his own cars. Childress would run the show, Dale would drive the cars, former crew chief Doug Richert would be

Dale holds the winner's trophy under a steady downpour at Darlington International Raceway after the 1987 Southern 500. (Charlotte Observer)

a crew member and former team owner Bud Moore would be the car builder.

Childress would go on through the years to transform Dale from country boy from Kannapolis into an empire. But Dale had another important issue to take care of.

Being a daddy.

In June, Dale, who was divorced, received custody of his children, Kelley, 9, and Dale Jr., 7.

"It meant so much," he said. "I love those hugs and kisses."

Dale prepares to run a couple of practice laps in 1983. (Charlotte Observer)

Racing through the 1980s

For someone who had just been Rookie of the Year and Winston Cup champion, Dale Earnhardt found 1981 was not a good year. In 31 races, Dale had 17 top-10 finishes, but he never won a race and he never won a pole. It was almost as if he had to prove himself all over again.

"Didn't Richard Petty go almost two years without a winning a race?" he asked a reporter.

Dale shows the ambition and the competitiveness it takes to become a successful race car driver. (Charlotte Observer)

Even though his team was going through change after change, the fans expected their favorite driver to keep winning.

Dale did better in 1982 and 1983. In April 1982, he was back in Victory Lane, celebrating at

Darlington with his children and his new wife, Teresa.

In 1983, he won two races in 30 starts—at Nashville and Talladega—had 14 top-10 finishes and won $446,272.

He almost had to give $10,000 of it back.

Dale, whose technique behind the wheel would make a driver's ed teacher crazy, ignored a black flag in the Clash, a special race at Daytona, for 11 of 22 laps. A black flag means a driver must get off the track and return to the pits, and Dale was ordered in because his car had an oil leak. But Dale didn't want to pit.

"I race under NASCAR rules, but the Clash isn't a regular race," he said later. "If it had been, I would have pitted. The Clash has always been presented to me as sort of a no-holds-barred deal."

He was fined $10,000.

But Dale, always one to try to persuade people to see things his way, got his message across to NASCAR officials. Two days later, the fine was cut to $5,000, with $2,000 of that to be returned if he behaved himself in the next 10 races.

"He's a high-strung thoroughbred," car builder Bud Moore said back then. "Dale has this urge to run over everything in his way to get to the front."

He did that a lot in 1984, with 22 top-10 finishes and victories in Talladega and Atlanta. And he did it in his new cars, the Chevrolets fielded by Richard Childress instead of the Fords of Bud Moore, who took on driver Ricky Rudd instead. It was with Childress that Dale took on his famous No. 3, which had been on Childress' car when he was a driver.

(Both Dale and Ricky would be sponsored by Wrangler jeans that year, with Dale taking on his black color scheme in June 1987 when his sponsorship was switched to Goodwrench and that company's colors.)

"I think in the long run the moves we made will prove equally good for both me and Ricky," Dale said of the switch.

It worked out fine for Dale, who went on to win four races in 1985 and five races in 1986.

But he didn't win the big one. The Daytona 500 in February always is the first race of the season, and it's the one Dale always wanted to win but —until 1998—never could.

In 1986, the way he lost at Daytona was almost too funny to be true.

With three laps to go, Dale was about an inch behind leader Geoff Bodine, right where he wanted to be. The plan was to wait until the last lap, then zip around Bodine and win the race.

It didn't happen.

He ran out of gas.

Dale dances around as he jokes with a TV cameraman in the NASCAR garage area at Daytona. (Charlotte Observer/Jeff Siner)

"I can take losing just like I can take winning," he said. "Ain't nothing to complain about. But now, the party's over."

He would find reasons for a party later that year, with victories at Darlington, North Wilkesboro, Charlotte twice and Atlanta.

And when the season was finished, Dale again gave credit to his daddy, Ralph.

"I stood on his tow truck as a boy, and I think I must have seen every lap he ever drove," Dale said. "I guess you could say I adopted his style of driving, and I've tried to capitalize on what he told me, all the advice he gave me. I wish I'd paid more attention."

Said Bud Moore, "The same fire is there in both father and son."

In 1987, Dale won 11 of 29 races and $2,099,243 and was Driver of the Year. His car was so hot that he won six of the first eight races of the season. But his swerving, "get-out-of-my-way" style was starting to get to some of the other drivers, which is understandable since everyone else was having a difficult time winning anything.

"When a man pulls over and lets you beside him, then tries to run you into the wall, is that racin'?" driver Bill Elliott wanted to know after a race in Charlotte that May.

Added driver Tim Richmond, "It was worth being in third just to watch the show. It was bumper cars that last 10 laps."

Elliott and Dale spent those last laps banging into each other, bending fenders and racing as if they were on the wild dirt tracks back in Ralph Earnhardt's day.

"If he thinks that's racing, he's sick," said driver Geoff Bodine after being spun out in the heat of it all.

But Dale the Intimidator must have been having a good time.

Dale, 36 years old, also won in 1987 at Michigan; Pocono, Pennsylvania; Bristol, Tennessee; Darlington, South Carolina; and Richmond, Virginia.

In January 1988, he was honored in Charlotte as the National Motorsports Press Association's Driver of the Year for 1987.

Dale ended the decade with several more wins —three in 1988, with 19 finishes in the top 10, and five in 1989, including 19 more top-10 finishes.

But there was something else special about the end of the 1980s. In July 1989 at the Florence Country Club in South Carolina, the National Motorsports Press Association Hall of Fame had a ceremony to induct Ralph Earnhardt.

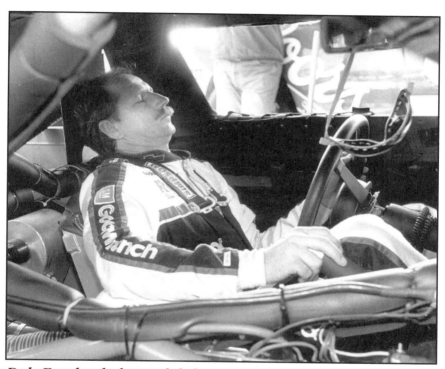

Dale Earnhardt dozes while his crew works on his car in the pits.
(Charlotte Observer)

"Everyone in the family loved to watch Daddy race," Dale said then. "I know this means a lot to my mother and my brothers and my sisters, and I can't begin to say how much it means to me."

The First Eight Races of the 1987 Season

Race	Winner	Dale's Finish
Daytona 500	Bill Elliott	5th
Goodwrench 500	Earnhardt	1st
Miller High Life 400	Earnhardt	1st
Motorcraft 500	Ricky Rudd	16th
TranSouth 500	Earnhardt	1st
First Union 400	Earnhardt	1st
Valleydale 500	Earnhardt	1st
Sovran Bank 500	Earnhardt	1st

Dale sits in his car in the garage area in 1988 at Charlotte Motor Speedway during practice. (Charlotte Observer)

You're Kidding, Right?

Driving a race car for a living is serious business. Drivers sometimes kid each other in the pit area or the garages, and most of them are friends. But when you're behind the wheel of a stock car going almost 200 miles per hour, it isn't time to joke around.

Unless you're a fan on a mission.

Dale did so well toward the end of the 1980s that someone thought he deserved a visit from . . .

the boogie man. It was the first of two bizarre incidents involving Dale, the second coming in 1989.

During NASCAR races, the tracks' infields are packed with fans in motor homes and trailers—fans who often come several days before a race to set up camp and hang out. Many times, the infield looks as if the fans who tag along from race to race have set up a tiny city. They bring their grills, their lawn chairs, inflatable swimming pools, their bicycles . . . whatever they need to feel at home for a few days.

In May of 1988, a man named Billy Wood—a fan of drivers Darrell Waltrip and Geoffrey Bodine—decided Dale had had enough good luck on the track, so he showed up at the Charlotte race to fix that.

Billy Wood thought he was the boogie man. He believed that by standing in front of the infield media center during a race, focusing his stare on a driver and raising his arms parallel to the ground, fingers crossed, he could control a speeding car.

So Billy Wood, in his pretend way, planned to have Bodine win the 300-mile race. He went through his moves. He focused on Dale. But on Lap 105, Dale moved up on Bodine's car, and suddenly, Bodine was spinning into the grass, out of the race.

Billy Wood was not happy. "You see what he did to my man!" he shouted.

Billy Wood was happy, however, when he learned that on Lap 198, two laps from winning the race, Dale's car suddenly blew an engine and Dale, too, was out.

The second weird incident came in September 1989, when Dale won his only pole that year. Thing is, Dale was never in the car.

Dale heads to Victory Lane after winning the second 125-mile race at Daytona in 1994. (Charlotte Observer)

Qualifying was being held in Martinsville, Virginia, and Dale was the leader in the points standings and was trying for his fourth Winston Cup championship.

But Hurricane Hugo had hit the Charlotte region, and Dale's farm in nearby Iredell County was damaged. He had to take care of the animals. He had to put fences back up before he could leave. "Everything is torn up around my house," he said when he finally got to the track.

So a guy named Jimmy Hensley, described as a down-on-his-luck local driver, was asked by Dale's crew to qualify the car. Hensley took that Chevrolet for a fast ride and beat Darrell Waltrip for the pole by 18-thousandths of a second.

"This just shows how strong Earnhardt's car really is," Waltrip said.

Strange.

Dale couldn't get stopped in the pits and was disqualified in his try for the pole in the 1998 Winston. (Charlotte Observer)

The 1990s: Chicken Bones and a Champion

Racing historian Bob Latford once said, "Dale would have made a good cowboy, a gunfighter." It's in his racing style, Latford said, which resembles that of North Carolina racing legend Junior Johnson. "Hard-charging, running for the front and don't worry about the sheet metal," Latford said.

But sometimes, even a 3,500-pound race car is no match for a chicken bone.

The 1990 season started the way most had for Dale, with a close-but-no-win in the Daytona 500, the one race he always wanted to win. Less than a mile from the finish line, Dale was leading, but suddenly at the end of the backstretch, he cut a tire. "I heard it hit the bottom of the car and then it hit the tire and the tire went," Dale said.

The bleachers back there sometimes are called the chicken bone seats, because they don't cost as much and fans often bring along their own food. Everyone thought he ran over a piece of chicken thrown onto the track. Turns out it was a piece of metal, but still …

When the race ended and Derrike Cope had won, Dale sat still in his car for more than a minute. No one bothered him.

"I never thought I had it in the bag," he finally said.

But things would get better. Dale won nine races that year and more than $3 million, but the best part was winning his fourth Winston Cup championship. When he was honored at the year-end banquet at New York City's Waldorf-Astoria Hotel in the grand ballroom, it was special.

"Friday night was the warmest in New York for me for a lot of other reasons, one of them being that it was the first time my mama, Martha, got to come to the Waldorf and be at the awards program in person," he said. "Her being here means a lot to me. I just wish Daddy could have been, too, 'cause he has never left my heart."

His speech that night, 17 years after his daddy, Ralph, died, was filled with credit for the man who taught him about race cars.

Dale raises his arms in celebration after winning the second of two Gatorade Twin 125 races in 1998. (Charlotte Observer/Jeff Siner)

"I think I watched every foot of every lap he ever ran after I started going to races with him and Mom," Dale told the crowd. "And I was almost always at his elbow there in the garage in the back of our yard, trying to see what he did that made his cars so strong."

Dale learned. He won his fifth Winston Cup title and four races in 1991, and longtime *Charlotte Observer* NASCAR reporter Tom Higgins published a column that asked the question: Is Dale the best driver ever?

Dale's response was typical. "I never thought about being the best or greatest," he said. "I just wanted to drive a race car like my daddy."

In 1992, Dale had only one victory and took on a new crew chief, Andy Petree.

In 1993, though, he won his sixth Winston Cup title, putting him only one behind all-time leader Richard Petty. He also saw the next genera-

Dale appears pleased as he leans on the roof of his Chevrolet Monte Carlo before the start of the 1995 Southern 500 at Darlington. (Charlotte Observer)

tion of superstars coming up behind in his rear view mirror: Jeff Gordon was one.

Gordon was starting to become popular among the fans, and his racing skills were compared to

Dale's by car owner Rick Hendrick. "He's got a lot of Dale in him," Hendrick said of Gordon back then. "They both smell it when it's close and they want to go for it."

In July 1993, Dale let the fans see a different side of him—not the hard-running racer, but the man who can show sympathy for other drivers as people, not just competitors.

He won a race at Pocono Raceway, but it was what he and second-place finisher Rusty Wallace did after the race that mattered most.

The previous Tuesday, driver Davey Allison had died from injuries suffered in a helicopter crash. Three months earlier, driver Alan Kulwicki had died in a plane crash.

After the Pocono race, on the "cool-down" lap, Wallace circled the track slowly, waving a No. 28 flag—Allison's number—from the window of his race car. Dale pulled into the pits, where his crew handed him an even larger No. 28 flag. The crew knelt around the car and prayed. Then, Dale circled the track clockwise, opposite the direction drivers usually race, waving the flag. It was a "Polish victory lap," honoring both Allison and Kulwicki.

The crowd was silent.

In 1994, Dale tied Richard Petty by winning his seventh Winston Cup title. He had four wins and an incredible 20 top-five finishes. So did he go to Las Vegas to celebrate, like he did when he won his first title in 1980?

No way.

He flew to New Mexico to ride horses into the wilds of an Indian reservation to join an elk hunt.

"I'm getting away," he told reporters. "My Indian friends don't care anything about racing."

After all the smiles that came with 1994, the following year started off like any other. Dale failed to win in his 17th try at Daytona. Some people joked that for him to ever win it, officials would have to change it to the Daytona 499.

"This is the Daytona 500, and I reckon I'm not supposed to win the thing," he said.

He did win five races that year, but the new kid—Jeff Gordon—won the Winston Cup title. A rivalry was beginning, especially among their fans. It became their unwritten rule: You can wear black and support Dale, or wear rainbow colors and support Gordon, or you can support another driver, but you cannot support both Dale and Jeff Gordon.

"I think an upstart rivalry is good for the sport," Dale said.

Away from the track, the two were quite different. Dale lived on a farm, Gordon in a South Florida mansion. Dale wore jeans and cowboy

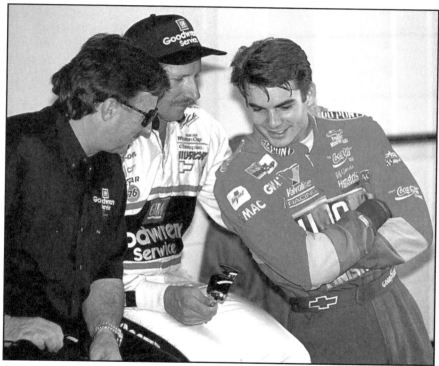

Jeff Gordon talks racing with Dale and Richard Childress in the garage area prior to the 1995 Winston Select. (Charlotte Observer/Christopher A. Record)

boots; Gordon likes designer clothes. Dale liked to go hunting; Gordon likes video games.

"I get along with Jeff, but we don't travel in the same circles," Dale explained.

Dale Earnhardt's and Richard Petty's Winston Cup Titles

EARNHARDT

Year	Races	Wins	Top 5	Top 10	Money won
1980	31	5	19	23	$588,926
1986	29	5	16	23	$1,168,100
1987	29	11	21	24	$2,069,243
1990	29	9	18	23	$3,083,056
1991	29	4	14	21	$2,396,685
1993	30	6	17	21	$3,353,789
1994	29	4	19	24	$1,453,370

PETTY

Year	Races	Wins	Top 5	Top 10	Money won
1964	61	9	36	41	$98,810
1967	48	27	38	39	$130,275
1971	46	21	28	41	$309,225
1972	31	8	25	27	$227,015
1974	30	10	22	23	$299,175
1975	30	13	21	24	$378,865
1979	31	5	23	27	$531,292

Dale was one of the greatest drivers in NASCAR's first half century. (Charlotte Observer)

Dale the Outdoorsman

Dale Earnhardt would tell you that you have to know where the big bucks are to get some, and that it's very seldom they will come to you. He also would have told you that to get big bucks, you have to smell right.

And he wouldn't have been talking about money.

One of Dale's favorite hobbies was hunting, and—as with most everything else in his life—there was a connection to his daddy, Ralph. Dale and

Ralph and their bird dogs would hunt together when Dale was a kid. A few weeks after Ralph died in 1973, Dale found it difficult to look at those dogs because of all the memories of his dad, so with his mother's permission, he sold them.

"They'd make me think of all the good times we'd had hunting together, and it was too much for me," he said. "I was only about 20 then, and I couldn't handle it."

Dale continued to hunt, however, probably as a tribute to his dad.

One of his biggest thrills came in 1984, when his best season wasn't on a race track, but in the woods.

Dale and some of his friends had leased some hunting property in Chester County, South Carolina, and during the winter, Dale's neighbor had taught him to use a turkey caller. Bagging a big turkey usually takes practice—you don't do it on your first hunting trip. At least, most people don't.

After a race in Bristol, Tennessee, in April, Dale headed for Chester County. "I walked into the woods before daylight, and it was pitch dark," he said then. "I went ahead and got situated, with a good-sized pine at my back and an old blown-down cedar sort of in front of me. I was camouflage head to toe."

Dale made a few clucking sounds on a turkey call and immediately got an answer from a turkey. "Here he comes around the end of that blown-down cedar, his tail fanned out and his head thrown back. "Right then, raising that shotgun, was as excited as I've ever been."

He brought home an 18-pounder—a big bird.

His trick: "A day or two before going hunting, I put the clothes I plan to wear in a plastic trash bag. Then I throw a bunch of pine cones and leaves out of the woods in there and hang the bag outside

Dale sits in his car before qualifying in Charlotte in 1997. (Charlotte Observer/Christopher A. Record)

in the air. My clothing absorbs the smell of the pine cones and leaves.

"When I get up on the morning of the hunt, I avoid the kitchen, where breakfast is being cooked. I take a shower but don't use any deodorant, lotion or talc. I then fetch my clothes and put them on. When I get to my stand, I feel like I smell as natural, as much like the woods, as humanly possible."

Dale knew that it not only takes sense to be a good hunter, but it also takes scents.

Dale and his wife, Teresa, keep company with two of the fastest machines around, his race car and an Air National Guard F-15 jet fighter. (Charlotte Observer)

Meanwhile, Back at the Farm

Dale Earnhardt's career put him in another world from when he played with toy cars on Daddy's garage floor on Sedan Avenue in Kannapolis.

He won more than $40 million, more than anyone else in motor sports. He earned the respect and admiration of millions of fans worldwide. He owned a car dealership, did commercial endorsements and traveled constantly to special appearances and photo shoots.

He could have lived anywhere, gone anywhere, bought anything.

So where did Dale call home? Mooresville, North Carolina, a short drive from Kannapolis.

His family owns about 1,000 acres and lives on about 300 acres of it, raising cattle and chickens. There are a few horses, too, just for trail riding, which his 12-year-old daughter, Taylor Nicole, who was born in December 1988, enjoys.

Out front, on Highway 136, is the symbol of what Dale became: a huge garage complex and showroom, so large it has been nicknamed the "GarageMahal." There are three buildings, the main one measuring more than 100,000 square feet.

"It's just absolutely mind-boggling," said Humpy Wheeler.

But behind all the glitter and glamor, there was a man who was a daddy, a husband and someone who just happened to drive a car for a living.

Race historian Bob Latford said Dale "would have made a good cowboy."

When he was home, that's just about what Dale Earnhardt was.

Ralph would have been proud.

Dale battles Jimmy Spencer down the front stretch at Charlotte Motor Speedway during the 1995 UAW-GM 500. (Charlotte Observer/Christopher A. Record)

Small-town Hero

Dale Earnhardt won more than $40 million on the NASCAR circuit and is known around the world, with his picture and that of his No. 3 Chevrolet appearing on all forms of merchandise, from T-shirts and caps to pocket knives and soft drink cups.

But the man who became a walking corporation grew up in a totally different atmosphere, in the quiet farming community of Kannapolis, North Carolina, in a small, white house with red trim and a rocking-chair front porch at the end of Sedan Avenue. That house, where Dale's mother, Martha, still lives, had an old barn out back that Dale's daddy, Ralph, transformed into a cinder-block garage made of sweat, grease and history.

Ralph Earnhardt also drove race cars and was NASCAR national sportsman division champion in 1956. He had a 23-year career that started in 1949 on Easter Sunday and gave him 500 recorded victories.

"My earliest memory is of watching Daddy in a race," Dale once said. "Following in his footsteps is all I ever wanted to do."

That path began in the cinder-block garage, where Ralph prepared his cars for weekend races at area dirt tracks and Dale, then a toddler, would play with his toy cars on the floor, mimicking Daddy.

This was an advantage for Dale, although he couldn't have known it then. "Unlike today's race drivers, his father, when he was not in the shop, was home," said Lowe's Motor Speedway president Humpy Wheeler, who has known the Earnhardts since the beginning of their racing careers. "So Dale had a chance to see him, and that's how he knew he was going to be a race driver."

As much success as that old garage brought the Earnhardt family, it also was the sight of tragedy. Ralph Earnhardt died there, on September 26, 1973, of a heart attack while working on one of his cars. He was 45. He left behind his wife; daughters Kay and Cathy; and sons Randy, Danny and Dale.

In 1981, Dale reopened that old garage, using it to build his Pontiacs.

"Being there brought back a lot of memories that mean a lot to me," Earnhardt said then. "A bunch of mine and Dad's old friends who used to volunteer to help on the cars came back around again."

Dale climbs out of his car after qualifying for the 1994 Mello Yello 500. (Charlotte Observer/Diedra Laird)

Today, that 30-foot-by-50-foot garage is home to M&F Auto Reconditioning and Detailing, run by Frankie Baskins and Dale's brother-in-law, Mike. In many ways, it's still the same. Drive through Kannapolis, past the farms and barns and cattle, and the quiet little dot on the map where so much tradition was bred and nurtured still endures.

The business has been there since the late 1980s, with the partners renting the building from Martha. They have changed it some, added a few walls and a kitchen area, but the office that used to be Dale's remains intact and is cluttered with racing items. The kitchen sports Earnhardt cereal boxes and Sun-drop cola bottles with Dale's picture on the label.

In front of it, next to the gravel drive, in the white house, Martha watches all that has happened to her family. She is 70 years old and still the an-

Dale smiles as he talks to Jeff Gordon in the garage area in 1999 at Lowe's Motor Speedway during practice for pole night. (Charlotte Observer)

chor that holds the family together. She saw the 2001 Daytona 500 on television, and it was the little house on Sedan Avenue where the family first thought to gather after the tragedy.

In recent years, she attended two races annually, at Lowe's Motor Speedway in nearby Charlotte, but that was about it for the racing circuit.

The community is growing around Sedan Avenue. Chain drug stores and supermarkets are creeping closer. Kannapolis' population has grown from 24,900 in Ralph Earnhardt's prime to nearly 36,000 today.

"Those places in Ralph's day were black and white—no technicolor," Humpy Wheeler said. "People were very conservative. When Ralph told Martha he would race full-time, it was a big thing back then. He promised her he would never take money the family needed to exist and put it in a race car."

Dale and his son, Dale Jr., sit on the back porch of a transporter discussing Dale Jr.'s preparation for Carquest 300 Grand National qualifications. (Charlotte Observer)

Look out across the yard from the front porch, at the construction and the shopping centers and traffic, and it's easy to see how Kannapolis is changing.

The presence of big business doesn't please Martha, who sometimes has trouble just sitting on her porch without people—strangers—stopping by, wanting something.

Still, the house is a safe retreat for the Earnhardt clan. Her children, grandchildren and great-grandchildren stop in periodically. Christmas is always special, when all her children come to be with her.

And family values and respect for what Ralph Earnhardt accomplished remain important. The reason Dale Jr.'s race car sports a No. 8 is that it was Ralph's number, and when Dale Sr. would tell a racing story, it often began with, "One time when my daddy," or, "I remember when Daddy . . ."

And when he was home on Sedan Avenue, Dale was just one of the kids. No one unique. Just Martha and Ralph's son, somebody's brother, somebody's uncle.

Martha Earnhardt has considered moving. Dale offered to find her a place. But she hesitates. The eight-room house in which she's lived for about 46 years, and which belonged to Ralph Earnhardt's parents before that, used to be 10 rooms, but the family needed more space and took out some walls. Now, Martha only uses the downstairs portion, with the upstairs for storage. She doesn't need even that much.

All the family lives nearby. The home is like a magnet for them, a piece of security in a changing world. Dale Jr., who calls Martha "Mammaw," once told her that she couldn't sell the house because it is what holds the family together.

Recalls Dale's public relations manager John "J. R." Rhodes: "I remember Dale when he was a little boy. In 1975, he was pretty raw in most matters of speaking, off and on the track. His dad's death, that knocked a lot of wind out of his sails."

Dale agreed. "It has been a long time, but he's still an everyday thought," he said not too long ago. "Whenever I have a problem, inside the race car or out, I still think, 'How would he have handled this situation? What would he have done?'

"He's still a big part of me."

Ralph would have liked that.

Dale sprays the Victory Lane crowd with champagne after winning the 1993 Winston at Charlotte Motor Speedway. (Charlotte Observer)

No Fear

Dale Earnhardt was not afraid of a race car. He was not afraid to go a little too fast, to bump and run, to pass without enough room.

When asked by an interviewer once what he was afraid of when driving, Dale thought for several moments. Finally, he said, "Fire." There always is concern about fire in a race car.

But Dale was never afraid of being in a wreck, and he had his share of them. He didn't like restrictor plates, which made the cars go slower on superspeedways. The Intimidator? Scared? That wouldn't be right. Compared to the ways cars used to run—at 200-plus miles an hour—building them to go slower made it seem, he said, like driving to Sunday school.

And he didn't like—and didn't use—the HANS device, a gadget that straps down a driver's helmet to prevent sudden head and neck movement.

He just wanted to race. Fast. Like his daddy did on the dirt tracks. Like his son does on high-banked asphalt.

In 1997, Dale was in a crash at Talladega that could have killed him. Humpy Wheeler remembers that July afternoon in Alabama.

"You could look down pit road and have a sense that something had happened and maybe he was dead," Wheeler said. "The thing we always fear is, 'What if a driver gets hit with his car upside down?' And this one ended up on its side, and no one could survive the kind of wreck he had."

Dale had been battling Sterling Marlin for the lead when Marlin's car and Ernie Irvan's car touched and Marlin's sent Dale into the wall. The car flipped on its side and was hit in the roof by the car of Derrike Cope. It took safety crews several minutes to get Dale out. Seemingly, none of the estimated 100,000 spectators moved or spoke. Amazingly, Dale walked to the ambulance by himself. Doctors said he had chest pains and a fractured chest bone and collarbone.

"The reason he survived, and the only reason he survived, is that he did what everyone told him not to do," Wheeler said. "It's the slouching way he sits in a race car. Also, his seat is rigged up so his head leans toward the outside of the car.

"The fact that he walked out of that car is phe-nomenal."

On February 18, 2001, Dale didn't walk away.

On the last lap of the Daytona 500, he was running third behind eventual winner Michael Waltrip and his son, Dale Jr., both of whom race for Dale Earnhardt Inc. Despite his hard-charging reputation, Dale was doing something different— protecting the leaders and holding off traffic. Within seconds, Marlin's car and Dale's car touched, sending Dale's up toward the wall in front of Ken Schrader's Pontiac. Dale's Chevrolet slammed into the wall, then slid back across the track into the infield grass.

The ambulances came. Dale Jr. ran toward his dad. The car's roof was removed. Dale was sped to Halifax Medical Center. There were trauma teams and a neurosurgeon. It was 4:54 p.m. His wife was at his side. He was pronounced dead at 5:16.

Dale Earnhardt was buried in an undisclosed location on Wednesday, February 21, 2001, following a private family service. He was 49.

The next day, an invitation-only memorial service was held at Calvary Church in Charlotte.

Singer Randy Owen of the musical group Alabama sang "Goodbye (Kelly's Song)" and "Angels among Us." The Lord's Prayer was said, and scripture was read from the Book of St. John. Dale Beaver, a chaplain with Motor Racing Outreach, which ministers to race drivers, spoke of Dale as a caring father, someone who always wanted to make sure those around him were happy.

Dale, you succeeded in that.

Thanks for taking us along for the ride.

Dale Earnhardt Quick Facts

April 29, 1951 - February 18, 2001

Birthplace: Kannapolis, North Carolina

Home: Mooresville, North Carolina

Wife: Teresa

Children: Kerry, Kelley, Dale Jr., Taylor Nicole

Favorite food: Steak

Favorite sports team: Atlanta Braves

Favorite toys: 76-foot and 50-foot boats, a Learjet and KingAir 200 plane

Favorite charities: Motor Racing Outreach and Special Olympics

Favorite car: The No. 3 Goodwrench Chevrolet

Money in the bank, through 2000: About $40 million

Favorite victory: The 1998 Daytona 500. Finally.

Dale Earnhardt's Ride

Team: Richard Childress Racing

Owner: Richard Childress

Car Number: 3

Make: Chevrolet Monte Carlo

Sponsor: GM Goodwrench

Colors: Black, red and white

Crew Chief: Kevin Hamlin

Fuel System: 22 gallons

Tires: Goodyear Racing Eagles

Weight: 3,400 pounds

Horsepower: 700@800 rpm

Racing Superstar Series Titles

Collect Them All!

Football Superstar Series Titles
Collect Them All!

Only $4.95 per book!

**Call Toll Free: 1-877-424-BOOK (2665) or
visit us at www.sportspublishinginc.com**

Basketball Superstar Series Titles
Collect Them All!

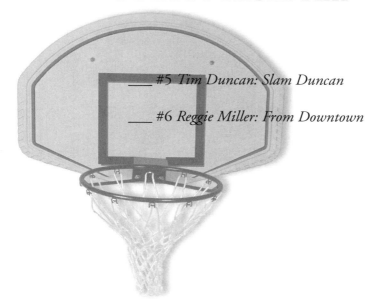

___ #5 *Tim Duncan: Slam Duncan*

___ #6 *Reggie Miller: From Downtown*

Only $4.95 per book!

Baseball Superstar Series Titles

Collect Them All!

____ *Mark McGwire: Mac Attack!*

____ *#3 Randy Johnson: Arizona Heat!*

____ *#5 Bernie Williams: Quiet Superstar*

____ *#7 Mo Vaughn: Angel on a Mission*

____ *#8 Pedro Martinez: Throwing Strikes*

____ *#9 Juan Gonzalez: Juan Gone!*

____ *#10 Tony Gwynn: Mr. Padre*

____ *#11 Kevin Brown: Kevin with a "K"*

____ *#12 Mike Piazza: Mike and the Mets*

____ *#13 Larry Walker: Canadian Rocky*

____ *#15 Sandy and Roberto Alomar: Baseball Brothers*

____ *#16 Mark Grace: Winning with Grace*

____ *#17 Curt Schilling: Phillie Phire!*

____ *#18 Alex Rodriguez: A+ Shortstop*

____ *#19 Roger Clemens: Rocket!*

____ *#23 Jim Thome: Lefty Launcher*

Only $4.95 per book!

Call Toll Free: 1-877-424-BOOK (2665) or visit us at www.sportspublishinginc.com